But, You're a Duck

By Michael Teitelbaum
Illustrated by Rose Mary Berlin

To Nicholas and Regina:
For keeping the child within you alive;
and
To Sheleigah:
For keeping the child in me alive.

A GOLDEN BOOK • NEW YORK
Western Publishing Company, Inc., Racine, Wisconsin 53404

MCMXCII

It was a warm spring afternoon in New York City. Merle, the landlady, was in the basement of her apartment building feeding her pets. Merle loved animals. She took in stray dogs and cats and gave them a good home.

Today there was quite a surprise waiting for her. "It's a little baby duck!" said Merle. "You must have been someone's Easter present, but then you got lost. Poor thing."

Merle instantly fell in love with the duck. It was so sweet and scared that it reminded Merle of the way she felt when she was a little girl in the big city.

"I'm going to keep you," Merle said to the duck. "And I'm going to call you Fiorello!" Fiorello was the name of the Mayor of New York when Merle was a little girl.

Merle fed and cared for Fiorello. In no time the duck grew big and happy.

"It's time for your walk, Fiorello," said Merle as she attached his leash to his collar. She had trained him to walk with her.

The sight of a duck on a leash out for a walk in New York City was very unusual indeed. Every day, during their walk, people on Merle's street pointed and smiled at Fiorello.

One day two of the neighborhood children,
Nicholas and Regina, spotted Merle and Fiorello out
for their walk. The children lived on Merle's block in
the city, but they also had a country home where
they went on weekends.

"What a sweet-looking duck!" exclaimed Regina.

"He sure doesn't act like a duck!" said Nicholas.
"I don't think this duck even knows he's a duck!"

"You're a duck, Fiorello!" shouted Regina. Fiorello
just rubbed against her leg and quacked happily.

One morning Merle was very busy working in
her building.

"Would you take Fiorello along on your walk?"
Merle asked her neighbor, who was walking his
three dogs.

Everything was fine until the dogs spotted three
cats. The dogs pulled to go in different directions,
and in the confusion Fiorello broke loose from
his leash.

Fiorello was terrified. He had never been away from Merle before, and now he was lost in the big city. Fiorello dashed down a flight of stairs and ended up on a crowded subway train.

"Look, it's a duck!" exclaimed one surprised passenger. Others stared or laughed.

"Mommy, can we take him home?" asked one little girl.

But before the little girl's mother could answer, the train stopped, the doors opened, and Fiorello ran up the stairs—right into Bloomingtail's department store!

Fiorello ran through the store flapping his wings and quacking at the top of his lungs. "Excuse me," one customer said to the manager. "Did you know that there's a duck in the store?"

"Don't be silly," replied the manager. "How can there be a—" He never finished. The manager spotted Fiorello and chased him through the store.

Fiorello dashed through a rack in the children's department. He came out the other side with a shirt around his neck. As Fiorello passed the ladies' department a startled customer knocked over a hatstand. One of the hats landed on Fiorello's head.

Fiorello headed for the door.

When he stumbled out onto the street, he was dressed in a child's shirt and a lady's sun hat!

The poor frightened duck continued to run. Fiorello was headed toward Central Park, one of the largest parks in the city.

Fiorello kept running through Central Park and fell right into a big fountain. A typical duck would have felt safe in the water, but Fiorello had never learned how to swim and was drowning.

"Look! There's a duck in the fountain, all dressed up in clothes!" someone yelled.

"Now I've seen everything!" added someone else.

"Well, what have we got here?" asked a passing police officer, who pulled Fiorello from the water. "An address tag on your collar, huh? We'd better get you home!"

Merle was very relieved when she opened her door to find the police officer carrying the soaking-wet duck.

"City's no place for a duck, ma'am," said the police officer. "Country's the place for a duck. Country, ma'am."

As Merle cleaned and fed Fiorello she thought about what the police officer had said.

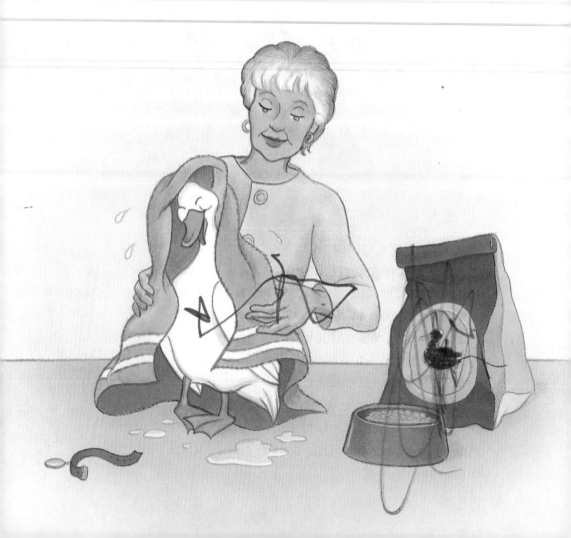

The next morning Nicholas and Regina came to
see Merle again. She told the children about
Fiorello's adventure, and about what the police
officer had said.

"Why doesn't he come and live with us at our
country home?" asked Regina.

"You can visit him anytime you like," offered
Nicholas.

Merle agreed. Although she would miss Fiorello,
she knew that the country was the place for a duck.

And so, Fiorello left the hustle and bustle of the big city for a new life in the country.

Nicholas and Regina left Fiorello outside and went into their house. "Now you play outside, Fiorello!" said Regina. "Try and get used to the place."

But the duck just paced back and forth in front of the door and scratched on the screen with his beak. He was used to being around people, and he just didn't know how to act like a country duck.

Nicholas let Fiorello into the house. He waddled
over to a basket of laundry and curled up in it like a
lazy old dog.

"You're a duck, Fiorello!" yelled Regina. "Go
outside and swim in our pond!"

"But he doesn't know how to swim!" said
Nicholas.

"Let's teach him!" said Regina.

The children figured that they would start off simply. They took Fiorello upstairs and put him into the bathtub. The duck flapped his wings, quacked a few times, and then scrambled to get out of the tub.

"If we take him outside to the pond, we can go into the water with him," said Nicholas. "That way we can show him it's safe."

They put on bathing suits and jumped into the
pond. Fiorello leaned over the edge of the pond and
stared at his reflection. No matter how much the
children called to him, Fiorello would not go into
the water.

"I think I know what Fiorello's problem is," said
Regina, watching the duck stare at his reflection. "He
needs to see other ducks!"

Nicholas and Regina then took Fiorello to a nearby lake where many other ducks lived. "Go on, Fiorello," coaxed Regina. "Go play with the other ducks." But Fiorello didn't want to leave the two children.

Another duck came waddling over and looked at
Fiorello curiously. Fiorello looked back, amazed. The
new duck began to walk back toward the lake.
Fiorello turned and looked at Regina, who smiled.
"It's OK," she said. "Go ahead. You're a duck,
Fiorello! You belong here."

Very slowly, Fiorello followed his new friend
down to the edge of the lake. At first he stood there
watching the other ducks swimming and splashing.
Then Fiorello slipped into the water. Several of the
other ducks helped show Fiorello how to paddle and
stay afloat. Soon he was swimming with the others.

As the children watched Fiorello swim in the lake, they were happy for him. They also felt a little sad. "I'm going to miss him," said Regina.

"We can come here and visit him anytime!" said Nicholas. That made Regina feel better. They waved good-bye and left the lake.

A week later Merle came up to the country to visit
Nicholas and Regina. "Where's Fiorello?" she asked.
"Come on," said Nicholas. "We'll show you."
When the three friends arrived at the lake, they all
looked around, searching for Fiorello. It was Merle
who spotted him. "There!" she shouted.

When Fiorello saw his three old friends he ran
over to them, quacking with glee. After a short visit,
Fiorello ran back to the lake and swam around with
his new friends.

"He looks very happy," said Merle. "I'm so glad
he's finally found a home!"

"You *are* a duck, Fiorello!" shouted Regina. "And
now *you* know it, too!"